HODDER CHILDREN'S BOOKS

First published in Great Britain in 2012
by Hodder and Stoughton

This paperback edition published in 2017

A CIP catalogue record for this book
is available from the British Library.

ISBN: 978 1 444 94906 3

10 9 8 7 6 5 4 3

Printed and bound in China

MIX
Paper from
responsible sources
FSC® C104740

Hodder Children's Books
An imprint of Hachette Children's Group
Part of Hodder and Stoughton
Carmelite House
50 Victoria Embankment
London EC4Y 0DZ
An Hachette UK Company

www.hachette.co.uk
www.hachettechildrens.co.uk

FOR LEO BRANKO AND NIKA SUNAJKO

...AND TO MONIKA AND LUKA IN THE HOPE THEY WILL SOON BREAK THOSE SEEMINGLY UNBREAKABLE SLEEPING HABITS OF THEIRS.

www.davidmelling.co.uk

www.huglessdouglas.co.uk

HUGLESS DOUGLAS
and the BIG SLEEP

David Melling

Rabbit's House

Hodder Children's Books

Douglas was packing all his things for Rabbit's sleepover. He had a lot of stuff but there was plenty of room at Rabbit's. He packed his honeybee pyjamas, a toothbrush and a storybook.

He was very excited!

'I hope Rabbit reads a bedtime story,' thought Douglas as he set off into the woods. His bag was very heavy with all his things. First he got stuck and then he got lost.

He climbed up the nearest tree to see where he was.
Only the tree he chose was quite thin and...

...very

...very

...bendy!

Douglas crashed to the ground and nearly squashed
Little Sheep!

'Hello,' said Douglas. 'I'm going to Rabbit's
for a sleepover, but I'm lost.'

'I know the way,' Little Sheep squeaked.

Douglas smiled. 'Why don't you come along too?
THERE'S PLENTY OF ROOM AT RABBIT'S.'

Douglas scrambled out of the bush and brushed himself down.

'Funny,' he thought, 'my bag feels even heavier now.'

At last they arrived at Rabbit's house.
'Twooooooo twit! You won't fit!' Owl hooted.

'I only brought one little friend,'
said Douglas, 'and there's plenty
of room at Rabbit's.'

Rabbit's
House

'What about us?' cried the sheep.

Rabbit was very happy to see everyone.
'I love having sheep over for sleepovers,' she laughed,
and she waved them all into her house,
one by one by one.

'Your front door does look small,' baaed Little Sheep.
'Nonsense!' said Rabbit. 'There's plenty of room.'

Poor Douglas.

They pushed…

…and they pulled.

'I don't think this is working,' Douglas said.
'Wait a minute!' cried Rabbit, snapping her fingers.
'I'll dig a bigger hole.'

'There now,' puffed Rabbit. 'Isn't that cosy?'
Douglas wasn't so sure.

'When are you going to read us a bedtime story, Rabbit?' asked Little Sheep.

'As soon as I get in,' Rabbit replied. 'Budge up!'

Everyone shuffled and nudged and squeeeeeeezed about.

'THERE'S NO MORE ROOM AT RABBIT'S!'
cried Douglas.

Little Sheep brushed his tickly fleece against Douglas' big round nose.

'AA-AA-AT...

Out popped the sheep, one... two... three...

four… five… six… seven… eight… nine… ten!

There were sheep all over the place.

Douglas gathered them together
and looked around.

'There's plenty of room out here,' he said.

yawwwwwn!

zzzzzzzzzzz

So Douglas and the sheep settled down and listened
to Rabbit read a story.
'Once upon a time,' Rabbit began, 'there was a big, big
sleepover...'
And, one by one, they all closed their eyes and fell asleep.

What would you pack for a sleepover?

Slippers

Glow-in-the-dark gadgets

Pyjamas

Blanket

Storybook

Toothbrush

Woolly socks

Teddy bear

Midnight snacks

Earphones

Cuddly toy

Comforter

Dressing gown

Musical alarm clock

Friend

THERE WERE TEN IN THE BED!

How many special toys do you like to take to bed with you at night?
Why don't you find ten of your favourite toys and act out
'There were ten in the bed'?
Who will be the last one left in bed?!

THERE WERE TEN IN THE BED

There were **TEN** in the bed
And the little one said,
"Roll over, roll over!"
So they all rolled over
And one fell out...

There were **NINE** in the bed
And the little one said,
"Roll over, roll over!"
So they all rolled over
And one fell out...

There were **EIGHT** in the bed...
There were **SEVEN** in the bed...
There were **SIX** in the bed...
There were **FIVE** in the bed...
There were **FOUR** in the bed...
There were **THREE** in the bed...
There were **TWO** in the bed...

There was **ONE** in the bed
And the little one said,
"Good night!"